Sue Ellis worked in education for 36 years as a secondary teacher, a behaviour and attendance adviser, and lecturer at York St John University. She has a wide experience of listening to children's issues from the pupils she has taught and her own two children, Katie and Robert.

Now retired, Sue spends time visiting schools with her books *Gorgeous Gwendolen Goose and Other Stories* and *Proud Patrick Peacock and Other Stories*, encouraging children to be the best version of themselves. Sue was born in Liverpool, attended university in Reading and Oxford. She has lived in York since 1982.

THE LOST COAT

SUE ELLIS

Austin Macauley Publishers
LONDON · CAMBRIDGE · NEW YORK · SHARJAH

Copyright © Sue Ellis (2021)

The right of **Sue Ellis** to be identified as author of this work has been asserted by the author in accordance with section 77 and 78 of the Copyright, Designs and Patents Act 1988.

All rights reserved. No part of this publication may be reproduced, stored in a retrieval system, or transmitted in any form or by any means, electronic, mechanical, photocopying, recording, or otherwise, without the prior permission of the publishers.

Any person who commits any unauthorised act in relation to this publication may be liable to criminal prosecution and civil claims for damages.

A CIP catalogue record for this title is available from the British Library.

ISBN 9781528999533 (Paperback)
ISBN 9781528999540 (ePub e-book)

www.austinmacauley.com

First Published (2021)
Austin Macauley Publishers Ltd
25 Canada Square
Canary Wharf
London
E14 5LQ

With grateful thanks to the following people who all advised and guided me with this story:

- The pupils and staff that attended the Sheffield Wednesday Football Club Community Programme 'World Book Day' event in March 2019:

- Wharncliffe Side Primary School

- Hallam Primary School

- Pathways Primary Academy

- Malin Bridge Primary School

- Nether Green Junior School

- Shooters Grove Primary School

- Hillsborough Primary School

- Lowfield Primary School, Sheffield

- Our Lady Queen of Martyrs RC Primary School, York

- Sylvia Klays, senior teacher at St Aelred's RC Primary School, York

- Isobel Dunn, Premier League Coordinator at Sheffield Wednesday Football Club, who asked me to write a story for the community programme about knife crime and gang culture

- My wonderful family – my husband David Ellis, my children Robert Ellis and Katie Ellis Carrigg, and my parents Anita and Geoff Farrell, all who continue to be the wind beneath my wings.

- Deo Gratias.

The school playground was empty. The children hadn't arrived yet. The staff were busy behind closed doors, setting up for the wonderful day of learning ahead. All you could hear was the birds singing, and the distant hum of cars and lorries from the road. The smell of freshly-made cheese straws and apple pies, ready for break-time, drifted across the playground from the open window of the kitchens.

One by one, the children started to arrive. They kissed their mummies, daddies, grandparents and childminders goodbye and came into school, excited to be with their friends for the start of a brand-new day. A green coat was hung up on a peg in the cloakroom next to a black anorak.
'I'm so glad to be hanging up on the peg for a rest this morning,' sighed the green coat, 'we've already taken the dog for a walk, put the re-cycling out and been to the shops!'
'I was so relieved to get here on time,' replied the black anorak anxiously, 'we slept in and had to rush breakfast, but at least the bell hasn't gone yet!'
A red coat and a blue coat rushed in and were both hooked onto the pegs.
'We've already been swimming this morning! We were up at the crack of dawn!' they both exclaimed, 'we love swimming though! It's great fun!'
A pink coat with lovely shiny buttons was plonked on a peg. 'I'm so happy we are in school now,' the pink coat whispered. 'Our mummy and daddy have had a big argument this morning. We're pleased to get out of the house!'
'What happened?' enquired the green coat.

'Oh, just the usual,' replied the pink coat and the lovely shiny buttons began to quiver as the pink coat started to cry.

Bursting with excitement, a yellow coat with white spots arrived at the coat pegs. 'We're going to a birthday party after school! I can't wait! Birthday cake, fizzy pop and lots of games to play!! Yippee!'

A brown duffel coat, with wooden toggles on, rushed into the cloakroom and was dumped on the floor. 'Two games of football already in the playground and I am exhausted! I can't wait for lunchtime now until the next game!'

Dazed and dismayed, the brown duffel coat looked up at the other coats. 'I'm a topsy-turvy discombobulated duffel coat lying here! He-e-e-lp!' it cried, 'I want to be hanging on the hooks with the rest of you coats!'

The other coats chuckled at the helpless heap. Luckily, the next family came in and lifted the brown duffel coat onto a peg so nobody could stand on it. 'Phew!' said the brown duffel coat, 'at last, a comfortable place to rest and relax until lunchtime!'

Next, a bright purple coat with orange zig zags arrived but said absolutely nothing to the other coats. It hung silently on its peg and its hood drooped sadly. Coat by coat arrived in the cloakroom until all the pegs were full. Wellingtons, boots, shoes and trainers were all put in the racks down below. The school day had begun.

Later that day towards 3 o'clock, the coats started to stir and chatter among themselves.
'Nearly time to go to the birthday party,' exclaimed the yellow coat with white spots. 'I've got our present in my pocket!'
'Football practice now!' shouted the brown duffel coat with wooden toggles and it shivered with anticipation. The green coat started humming to itself, 'We're off to a piano lesson. I just love listening to the different tunes!'

'Netball practice for us!' declared the red and blue coats. The black anorak looked happy and was clearly looking forward to chilling out at Nana's and watching the television. The pink coat with lovely shiny buttons tried to put on a brave face but wasn't looking forward to going home. One by one, the children picked up their coats, book bags and water bottles, and left for home, except for the bright purple coat with orange zig zags. It was the last coat in the cloakroom. Nobody collected it and it hung from the hook looking all forlorn. The cleaners came and mopped the floor. As the sky got dark, the teachers left. Finally, the caretaker came and locked the doors, and the bright purple coat with orange zig zags was left on its own in the cold cloakroom for a long, lonely night.

The next day nobody came to pick up the bright purple coat with orange zig zags. The following morning the cleaner put it in the lost property box. It had no name tag on it and nobody seemed to know who it belonged to. It was offcially a lost coat. Day by day, other things were put on top of it in the box until it was completely hidden, lost and lonely. But the bright purple coat with orange zig zags was actually relieved to be in the lost property box because it was keeping a horrible, shameful secret. What on earth could that secret be?

The owner of the bright purple coat with orange zig zags, Sam, was hoping that everybody would forget about it. The coat was lost and that was that.
'Where is that bright purple coat with orange zig zags?' exclaimed mummy, 'It cost a lot of money!'
'Where is that bright purple coat with orange zig zags?' asked daddy, 'we bought it because we couldn't miss you in a crowd and now it's gone!'
Sam was ashamed about the secret it kept. The coat was in school somewhere but, if anybody looked in the pockets, there would be so much fuss. What was going to happen? The whole situation made Sam feel so sad and the tummy ache caused by the worry really, really hurt.

The following weekend Sam visited Grandma and Grandad's house. Just before they started reading their bed-time story, Sam started to cry. 'What would happen to me if I had made a terrible mistake, and my teachers and mummy and daddy found out?' asked Sam, 'I think they would be really cross with me.'

'It's always best to talk with your family about wrong choices you think you've made and then we can all help you sort it out,' replied Grandma wisely. 'There's nothing you have done that we haven't heard about before,' added Grandad in a calm, quiet voice.

'I have left my coat in school because in my pocket, right at the bottom, in a secret corner I have put a... a... knife*. One of the older children asked me to bring one into school if I wanted to be in their gang but I never showed them or told them. I have just ignored them and they have gone away.' The tears flowed freely now and Grandad fetched the tissues for them all to blow their noses!!!

'Well, I think tomorrow we can discuss all this with mummy and daddy,' replied Grandma. 'Then they can go into school with you to sort it out and find your lost coat. It will all be alright in the morning,' replied Grandma.

Sam slept better because the problem had been shared.
On Monday, mummy and daddy went into school early to find the lost coat and to talk with the class teacher. Everybody agreed you should never carry a knife as this could lead to big trouble. The bright purple coat with orange zig zags now hung proudly in the cloakroom and chattered contentedly with all the other coats. Sam was so relieved that the coat was now found and life could go on happily with friends and family.

'Always discuss your worries with us,' re-assured mummy and daddy with a smile.
'Remember,' said Grandma and Grandad on their next visit, 'a problem shared is a problem halved.'
And they were absolutely right!

(*Author's note – This story can be adapted to illustrate anything that a child is forbidden to bring to school)

CPSIA information can be obtained
at www.ICGtesting.com
Printed in the USA
LVHW072003150421
684636LV00022B/1285

P.M. Hillman is a full-time IT professional and proud mother of two grown sons. She loves animals, music, food and curling up with a good book. One day, she plans to visit Italy and see Venice. She lives in regional Victoria, Australia, with her family and several pets.

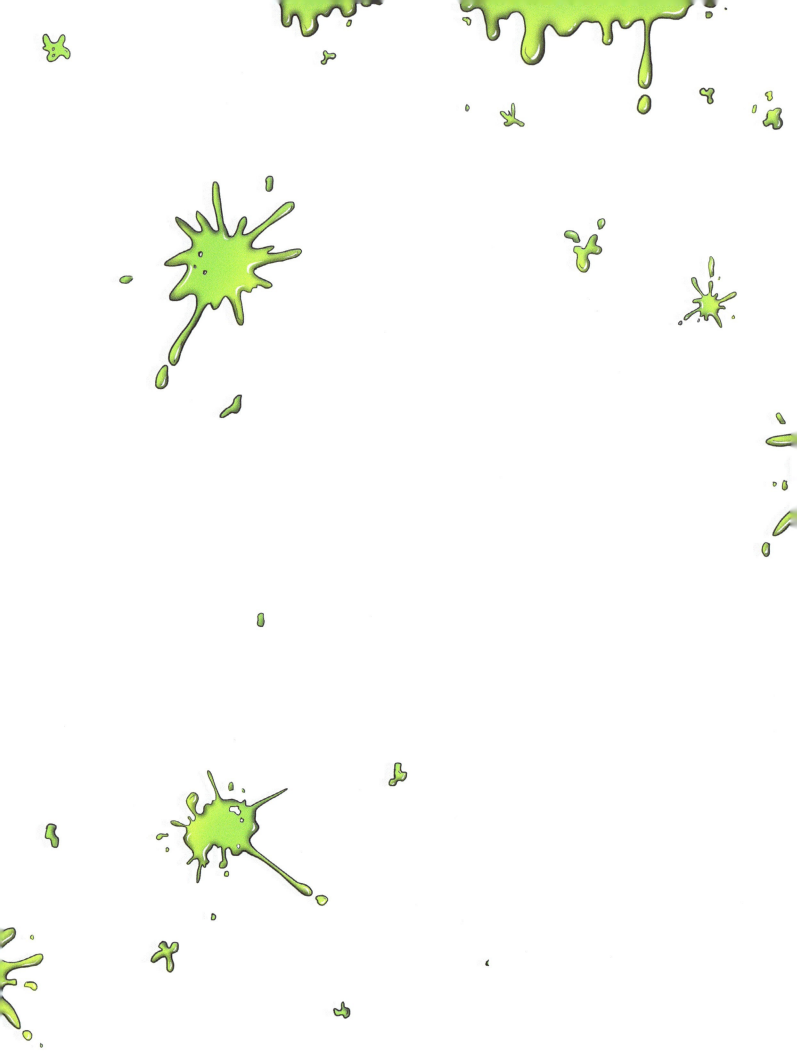

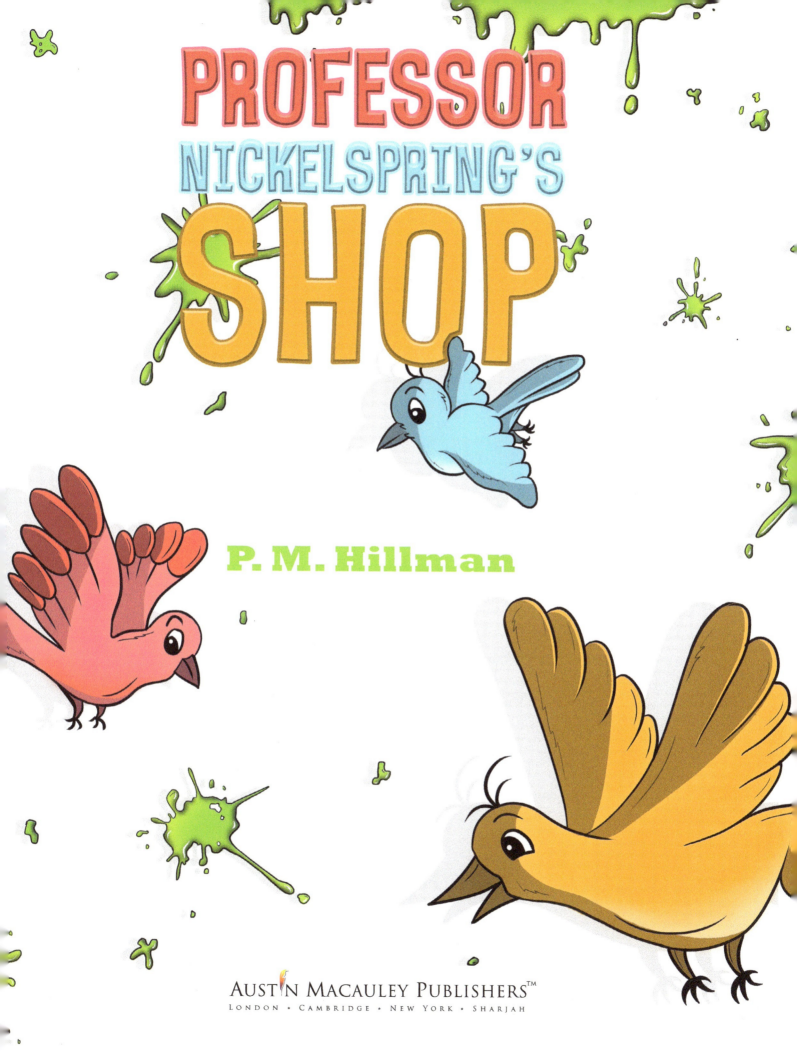

PROFESSOR NICKELSPRING'S SHOP

P. M. Hillman

AUSTIN MACAULEY PUBLISHERS
LONDON • CAMBRIDGE • NEW YORK • SHARJAH

Copyright © P. M. Hillman (2021)

The right of **P. M. Hillman** to be identified as author of this work has been asserted by the author in accordance with section 77 and 78 of the Copyright, Designs and Patents Act 1988.

All rights reserved. No part of this publication may be reproduced, stored in a retrieval system, or transmitted in any form or by any means, electronic, mechanical, photocopying, recording, or otherwise, without the prior permission of the publishers.

Any person who commits any unauthorised act in relation to this publication may be liable to criminal prosecution and civil claims for damages.

A CIP catalogue record for this title is available from the British Library.

ISBN 9781528996839 (Paperback)
ISBN 9781528996846 (ePub e-book)

www.austinmacauley.com

First Published (2021)
Austin Macauley Publishers Ltd
25 Canada Square
Canary Wharf
London
E14 5LQ

To my family.

Down the road and around the corner was a city called Bustlers Bend.

Each shopkeeper was very proud of their shop and thought theirs was the best in town.

There was one shop that was different, Professor Nickelspring's. He was an inventor; a good one too. But he didn't really care what his shop looked like.

Every morning as the professor walked to his shop, everyone would complain.

The professor would just smile and say, "It's not the outside but what happens on the inside that makes a shop wonderful."

No one understood.

One hot evening some visitors came to town. They had been flying for days and all those wonderful shops looked very comfortable. They decided to make themselves at home.

Can you imagine what the shopkeepers saw next morning? Apart from being noisy, birds are very messy. Can you guess what I mean? That's right, poop! Pretty soon all those beautiful shops were covered in piles of bird poo.

The shopkeepers weren't happy. Do you blame them? They agreed the birds had to go now! But how do you scare away so many birds?

Mr Crust, the baker, had an idea. Why not shoo the birds away with brooms?

Of course, your normal broom won't reach the top of a shop. So, Mr Hardwood from the tool shop helped by making really long handles for the brooms. The shopkeepers got to work. But the birds stayed put.

Next, Mr Crisp, the grocer, spoke up.

"I have a pile of old brussel sprouts and parsnips that we could throw at them," he said. "I can never seem to sell them."

Nobody bought them because everyone thought they tasted terrible! Secretly, they were all glad to be throwing them at the birds.

Now old vegetables are pretty squishy and smelly. Throwing them at a building just makes them splat everywhere. So, when the shopkeepers started throwing the vegetables,
the mess got bigger.
The birds jumped but they didn't go away.

Things were getting worse.

There was a town meeting. Mr Snout, the mayor, decided it was hopeless and they would all just have to leave town. They had no choice. Sadly, everyone agreed except Professor Nickelspring.

"Perhaps I can help," he said. "I have an idea that just might work. But it will take time."

The townspeople agreed to give it a try and Professor Nickelspring got to work.

Everyone waited anxiously. What could he do to help them?

Nobody could guess what he had invented. The Professor smiled and said, "I call it a scare-in-a-box."
From his pocket, he pulled out a remote control.
The townspeople were totally confused.

The whole town cheered! The birds were gone but the mess was terrible.

Once again, the shopkeepers could be proud of their shops. Professor Nickelspring's shop was still dingy and run-down but no-body cared anymore. Everyone knew that this was the best shop in the city.

THE END